Max and Zoe

at the Library

by Shelley Swanson Sateren

illustrated by Mary Sullivan

PICTURE WINDOW BOOKS

a capstone imprint

Max and Zoe is published by Picture Window Books
a Capstone Imprint
1710 Roe Crest Drive
North Mankato, Minnesota 56003
www.capstonepub.com

Library of Congress Cataloging-in-Publication Data
Sateren, Shelley Swanson.
  Max and Zoe at the library / by Shelley Swanson Sateren ;
illustrated by Mary Sullivan.
      p. cm. -- (Max and Zoe)
  Summary: Max learns the importance of taking good care of
library books, with help from his friend Zoe.
  ISBN 978-1-4048-6210-4 (library binding)
  ISBN 978-1-4048-8058-0 (paperback)
[1. Books and reading--Fiction. 2. Friendship--Fiction.
3. Schools--Fiction.] I. Sullivan, Mary, 1958- ill. II. Title.
  PZ7.S249155Max 2011
  [E]--dc22
                                    2011003725

Art Director: Kay Fraser
Designer: Emily Harris

Printed in the United States of America in Stevens Point,
Wisconsin.

092012   006937WZS13

Table of Contents

Chapter 1
Bugged by Buddy

Max and Zoe were

reading in Max's room.

"Woof!" Buddy dropped

a ball in Max's lap.

"Not now, Buddy. I'm at

the best part of the story!"

Max said.

"Woof!"

"Later, Buddy. Super Squirrel is saving the world," Max said.

"Woof! Woof!"

"Oh, okay." Max folded down a corner at the top of the page.

He stood up and threw
the ball. Buddy chased it.
Zoe picked up Max's book
and opened it.

"Max! You made so many
dog ears!" she said.

"I did what?"

he asked.

"You folded the corners,"

said Zoe. "Like tiny dog ears,

see? It ruins the books.

Ms. Kim said so."

"I never heard that.

Anyway, I can't lose my

place every time Buddy

bugs me," Max said.

"But you've ruined a library book AGAIN, Max," Zoe said.

"That other one was a total accident. It fell in the lake!" Max said.

"You had to pay Ms. Kim for that book," Zoe said.

Max groaned. "And I couldn't check out another book until I paid. Mom made me earn the money. It took three weeks!"

"If this book is ruined,

you won't get to check out

the next Super Squirrel book

tomorrow," Zoe said.

"That stinks!" Max said.

"Wait. I know what to do!"

Max pressed all of the

dog ears flat. Then he put

the book on the floor and

stood on it.

"Max! What are you doing?" Zoe asked.

"I'm ironing the wrinkles," he said.

"You better stop. I think you're making it worse," Zoe said.

Max got off the book and looked at the page corners. Little lines still showed.

"I just need more weight. You hold Buddy, Zoe. Then you get on my back," Max said.

Zoe and Buddy were

heavy. Max's knees shook.

He stepped onto the book

again.

Max wobbled.

Buddy jumped out of

Zoe's arms.

Max and Zoe fell onto
the rug.

"Are you okay?" Max
asked.

"Yeah. Did it work?" Zoe
asked.

"No. I'm in big trouble,"
Max said with a sigh.

The next day Max had library hour at school.

"Maybe Ms. Kim won't notice," thought Max. "It's not that bad."

Max waited in line to return his book. The girl in front of him was reading her book. It had dog ears inside, too!

Suddenly, Max had an idea.

Max showed his book to
Ms. Kim.

"Oh, dear. Max, this is a
mess. That will be another
five dollars," she said.

"But I have an idea," said

Max. "I could make a poster

for you instead of paying.

It could ask people not to

make dog ears in books."

"Okay, Max," Ms. Kim said. She took out some art supplies for Max.

Max worked hard on the poster. He made a bookmark for himself, too.

Then he checked out a new book.

That night, Max read the

next Super Squirrel story.

Buddy jumped on the bed.

"Woof!"

"Hang on a second,

Buddy," Max said.

Max marked

his page with his

new bookmark.

It was a picture

of a dog with big,

floppy ears.

No
Dog
Ears

"And Super

Puppy saves the place!"

he said.

"Woof! Woof!"

About the Author

Shelley Swanson Sateren is the author of many children's books and has worked as an editor and a bookseller. Today, besides writing, she works with children aged five to twelve in an after-school program. At home or at the cabin, Shelley loves to read, watch movies, cross-country ski, and walk. She lives in St. Paul, Minnesota, with her husband and two sons.

About the Illustrator

Mary Sullivan has been drawing and writing her whole life, which has mostly been spent in Texas. She earned her BFA from the University of Texas in Studio Art, but she considers herself a self-trained illustrator. Mary lives in Cedar Park, a suburb of Austin, Texas.

Glossary

accident (AK-si-duhnt) — something that happens by chance in which people are often hurt or things are broken

bookmark (BUK-mark) — a piece of paper or other flat thing used to mark a place in a book

dog ear (DAWG IHR) — the turned-down corner of a page in a book

fault (FAWLT) — a mistake

ruined (ROO-ind) — wrecked

wobble (WOB-uhl) — to move in a shaky way, from side to side

wrinkle (RING-kuhl) — a line or fold in something

Discussion Questions

1. The first time Max ruined a book it was an accident. His mom made him earn money to pay for the book anyway. Do you think that was fair? Why or why not?

2. Max learned not to make dog ears. In what other ways can you take good care of books?

3. Did you ever get in trouble for ruining something? What happened?

Writing Prompts

1. Most school libraries have rules. List three rules that your library has.

2. Max had to earn money to pay for the first book he ruined. Make a list of three things you would do to earn money.

3. Max loves the Super Squirrel books. Write a few sentences about your favorite book. Be sure to include the title and the author.

Hi MAX!

Make Your Own Bookmark

Max makes a bookmark out of paper. You can use many different kinds of flat things for bookmarks.

What you need:

- tongue depressor or large craft stick
- markers
- 2 wiggle eyes
- craft glue

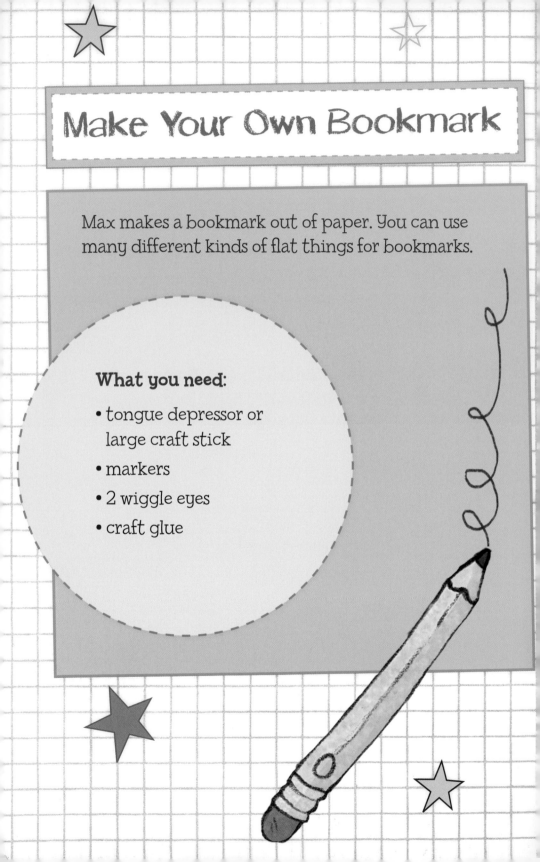

What you do:

1. Glue the wiggle eyes near the top at one end of the craft stick.

2. With the markers, draw hair and a nose. Also draw a silly or smiling mouth.

3. Now draw clothes, hands, and feet.

4. When the glue dries, use the silly bookmark to save your place.

HAPPY READING!

The Fun Doesn't Stop Here!

Discover more at www.capstonekids.com

- Videos & Contests
- Games & Puzzles
- Friends & Favorites
- Authors & Illustrators